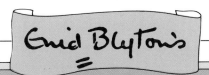

Enid Blyton's
Nursery~Rhyme Land

Illustrated by Kate Jaspers

SMITHMARK

Once upon a time there were twins called Tom and Polly.

They had dark curly hair, rosy cheeks, and blue eyes. They were happy children, always ready for a game and a laugh. And they were always looking out for an adventure!

One day the sun shone brightly, the birds sang, and the twins thought they would go out for a walk.

"Let's go somewhere that we've never been before," said Tom.

"Let's go right over the hill and down the other side. We might find an adventure!"

So off they went, running along in the sunshine. They climbed up the hill and set off down the other side. They came to a pretty lane, with white may on the hedges on each side.

"Let's go along here," said Polly.

They didn't meet anyone at all.

The cows in the field looked over the hedge at them, and some sheep baa-ed loudly. They could hear ducks quacking on a pond.

Just then they spotted someone coming toward them. It was a little girl, with a big crook in her hand. She was crying. Tom felt sorry for her.

"What's the matter?" he said.

"I've lost my sheep," said the little girl. "I suppose you haven't seen them, have you? There are about twenty of them."

"Well, we saw some sheep away back down the lane," said Tom. "They were baa-ing loudly. Perhaps they were yours."

"Oh, *thank* you," said the little girl, and hurried away, carrying her big crook. Polly turned and looked after her.

"Tom," she said suddenly, "do you know – I believe that was Little Bo-Peep!"

"Don't be silly," said Tom.

"Bo-Peep's only a nursery-rhyme person. That was a real girl."

They went on down the lane and suddenly came to a place where it divided into two. A big signpost stood there. And guess what? On one of its fingers was printed in big bold letters, "TO NURSERY-RHYME LAND."

"Goodness gracious!" said Polly, staring. "Look what that says, Tom. 'To Nursery-Rhyme Land.' Then that must have been Little Bo-Peep. I thought it was!"

"Polly – let's go to Nursery-Rhyme Land!" said Tom, excitedly. "It would be a real adventure! Let's go!"

"All right," said Polly. "But look, there's somebody sitting down by the signpost. I hope he'll let us go by."

As they walked past the signpost, the little man who was sitting there, reading a newspaper, got up. He stood in the middle of the lane and held out both his hands so that they could not get past.

TO NURSERY-RHYME LAND

"Only nursery-rhyme folk allowed this way," he said. "What are your names?"

"Mine's Tom," said Tom.

"And I'm Polly," said Polly. "Please let us pass."

"Well, I don't know which nursery-rhyme Tom you are, nor which Polly *you* are," said the man, "but those are nursery-rhyme names all right. You may pass. But let me warn you not to get into any trouble today, because the Old Woman Who Lives in a Shoe is in a very bad temper."

"Oh," said Polly, rather alarmed. But Tom pulled her on, past the little man. They ran on down the lane, and came to a little village. The children sat down on the edge of an old well, and watched the people going here and there.

"I'm sure these are all nursery-rhyme people!" said Polly, feeling really excited. "Tom, doesn't that

8

look exactly like Old Mother Hubbard? And look, she's got a dog following her – the one that was sad when the cupboard was bare."

"And isn't that Wee Willie Winkie?" said Tom, as a little boy ran past them. "He's still got his night-gown on! You know how the old rhyme goes:

> *'Wee Willie Winkie*
> *runs through the town,*
> *upstairs and downstairs,*
> *in his night-gown!'*

I suppose he always wears it!"

It really was fun watching all the people. Polly and Tom felt too shy to speak to any of them, but nobody took any notice of the twins on the well.

Suddenly a bell began to ring. It was twelve o'clock. Dinner-time! The people all hurried into their houses. "Ding-dong, ding-dong!" went the bell.

"Look," said Polly, "there's a boy coming. He's carrying a cat. He

9

doesn't look very friendly, does he? And isn't he thin?"

"He's coming here to the well," said Tom. The boy ran up to the well and pushed the twins aside.

"Get out of my way," he said rudely, and then, to the children's horror, he dropped the cat down the well! Splash!

"Oh, you bad boy!" cried Polly, and leaned over to see the poor cat splashing about in the water. The boy ran off, laughing.

"That's Johnny Thin, the nasty boy who put the cat into the well, in the rhyme," said Polly, almost in tears. "Tom, what can we do?"

"Let's go and knock on the door of the nearest cottage and get help," said Tom. So he ran to a nearby cottage, and knocked loudly.

A much fatter boy came to the door, smiling. "What's the matter?" he said. "Don't tell me the cat's down the well again!"

Tom recognized him as Johnny Stout.

"Yes, it is. Do come and get it before it's drowned!" begged Tom.

Johnny ran to the well with the others. He let down the bucket and the cat climbed into it. Then Johnny Stout wound up the bucket, and up came the cat. She at once jumped out, shook herself, and ran off.

"One of these days Johnny Thin will be caught by the Old Woman Who Lives in a Shoe!" said Johnny Stout. "She's always on the look-out for him – and for that bad Tom the Piper's Son, too. My word, when she catches them, what a telling-off they will get!"

A lovely smell came out of Johnny Stout's cottage. It made the children feel hungry. Johnny Stout noticed their hungry looks.

"Are you hungry?" he said. "I'm sorry I've no dinner to offer you, there's only the smell of it left now.

But you could go over to Jack Sprat's cottage, and ask Mrs. Sprat if she's got any food for you. Jack Sprat's away and there may be some meat left over. She won't eat any lean meat, you know."

Polly and Tom walked over to the trim little cottage near the green. Mrs. Sprat opened the door herself.

"We're rather hungry," said Tom. "I suppose you haven't any dinner to spare, Dame Sprat?"

"Bless your hearts, I've plenty!" said the plump old lady. "Jack Sprat's gone to market, and there's his share of the stew left. I've had mine. I pick out all the fat bits, you know, and he has all the lean ones. Come along in and eat."

They sat down and ate good helpings of a most delicious stew. Dame Sprat watched them, and then gave them some treacle tart. It was very good.

"What are your names?" she said. "I don't seem to know you – and I thought I knew everyone in this land. You must belong here, because no one is allowed in unless they are nursery-rhyme folk."

Polly and Tom turned red. They stared at the smiling old lady.

"My name's Tom," said Tom.

"What! You're surely not Tom, the Piper's Son!" cried Dame Sprat, and she looked angry. "I wouldn't have him in my house for anything, the rogue. He stole a pig, the rascal."

"No, I'm not that Tom," said Tom. "I'd never steal pigs or do things like that."

"Well, you must be Tommy Tucker, then!" said Dame Sprat. "Stand up and let me hear you sing! You sing for your supper, so you can sing for that large dinner you've had!"

"I can't sing," said Tom, and he turned red. "I go all out of tune. But Polly here sings nicely."

"Polly! Are you naughty little

13

Polly Flinders?" asked Dame Sprat. "Well, all I can say is I hope your mother punishes you if you go and sit in the cinders again! You two had better go home. I'm sure your mothers must be looking for you!"

Polly and Tom ran out, quite glad to get away from Dame Sprat's questions. They ran into a little wood that lay at the back of the village. Polly sat down on the grass. Then she pointed to something.

"Look, Tom," she said. "Someone has upset some milk and left it here with the bowl and spoon."

"Well – that must be Little Miss Muffet then," said Tom. "We'd better look out for the spider!" Just as he spoke, something dropped from a nearby tree, hanging on a silken thread. It was the biggest spider the children had ever seen in their lives!

The twins were not afraid of ordinary spiders – but this one was too big! It looked at them out of its

eight eyes, and it waved eight hairy legs in the air.

"Polly, run!" said Tom, and they ran. They bumped into a little girl hiding behind a tree. It was Little Miss Muffet.

"Has the spider gone?" asked Miss Muffet. "I want to get my bowl and

spoon. Oh no, there it is! Run!"

They all ran through the wood. They came at last to a road, and coming down it they saw soldiers riding on horses, with flags waving, looking very colorful.

"There go all the king's horses and all the king's men," said Miss Muffet.

"And there's Humpty Dumpty!" cried Polly, pointing to a large, egg-shaped person sitting on a wall. "I hope he won't fall!"

"He always does," said Miss Muffet. "He loves to give the soldiers a fright. There he goes, look! All broken into pieces, as usual!"

15

The horses reared up as Humpty Dumpty fell. Some of the soldiers tumbled off. Others ran to Humpty Dumpty, but they couldn't possibly mend him.

"He's stupid," said Miss Muffet. "He'll have to wait until Old Mother Hubbard comes by, now. She's the only one who can mend him. She knows a powerful spell."

The twins left Miss Muffet and followed the soldiers, trotting down the road. Soon they came to a palace. From inside there came the sound of fiddles playing a merry tune.

"Old King Cole has got his fiddlers three today," said one soldier to another. "Would you like to see him, children? He likes visitors."

Polly and Tom longed to go into the palace, of course, and see Old King Cole. So in they went, up a long, long flight of steps. Inside was an enormous hall, down the middle of which ran a large table. A meal was laid on the table, and Old King Cole was just about to seat himself at the head. Three fiddlers stood near him, playing merrily.

"Hallo, hallo!" he cried, as he saw the children. "Visitors! Splendid! Sit down, my dears, sit down. There's a pie coming in. Now, just let me see if I've got sixpence for you!"

He put his hand into his pocket and brought out a shiny sixpence. He gave it to Polly. Then he put his hand into his other pocket – and brought out a handful of rye seeds! He threw them down crossly.

"I've got my pocket full of rye again! Most annoying! Who puts it there, I'd like to know! Ah, here comes the pie. Good, I'm hungry. I hope it's a rabbit-pie!"

By this time the twins knew quite well what the enormous pie would be! Polly whispered to Tom.

"Sing a song of sixpence, a pocket full of rye, four and twenty blackbirds…"

"Stop whispering!" said Old King Cole. "Now – I'll give you a piece of this lovely pie!" He took up a large knife, and Polly called to him.

"Stop, Your Majesty! There are twenty-four blackbirds in that pie!"

"Nonsense!" said the King, and he put his knife into the crust. At once there came the flutter of many wings, and the flute-like whistle of blackbirds! And out of the enormous pie flew four and twenty blackbirds! They went to the window and flew out at the top. The king sat back in astonishment.

"Now, I won't have tricks like this played on me!" he cried. "Where's the queen? Fetch her at once!"

Nobody seemed to know where she was. Polly spoke up.

"She's in the parlor, eating bread and honey," she said. "Perhaps she knew it was only a blackbird pie, and thought she would rather have something else."

There came a sudden scream from the garden. Old King Cole jumped in alarm.

"That will be the blackbirds trying to peck off your maid's nose," said Polly.

Old King Cole banged on the table angrily.

"Who are these children who seem to know so much?" he roared. "Blackbirds in my pie! The queen eating bread and honey! Birds pecking my maid's nose! What next I should like to know! Bring me my pipe and my bowl and take these children to prison!"

Polly and Tom each gave a loud scream.

"Quick, Polly, run!" cried Tom, and took his sister's hand. The soldiers barred the way to the great front entrance of the palace, so the

children ran to another door. This led to the kitchens. They ran through them and out into the palace garden. The maid was sitting down there crying and rubbing her nose.

Down the garden path went the children and out of a gate in the palace wall. They didn't stop running until they were too out of breath to run any more. Then they sat down on a little hillside. Polly panted and Tom puffed. They both kept a sharp look-out for the soldiers.

After they had rested for a while, Tom and Polly went down the road again, wondering what was going to happen next! Really, it was very exciting to meet so many people they had only known before in their nursery rhymes.

A boy came running toward them. He looked frightened. He carried a fiddle in his hands, and tears were running down his cheeks.

"Oh!" he called, when he saw Tom and Polly. "Save me, save me!"

"What from?" asked Polly.

"From the farmer!" cried the boy. "I'm Tom the Piper's Son, and ever since I stole a pig from the farmer, he watches out for me and beats me when he catches me. I was just playing my fiddle in the market to get a few pennies when he saw me. There he comes now! Hold my fiddle for me, will you?"

He tossed Tom his fiddle and ran on, howling. A fat farmer appeared around the corner, glared at Tom and Polly, and went puffing after the other boy.

"What am I supposed to do with his fiddle?" said Tom, laughing. "Let's go on to the market, shall we? It sounds exciting. Tom the Piper's Son may come back there, and find us to get back his fiddle."

They walked on and came to the

market. Bo-Peep was there with her sheep. Little Boy Blue was there with his horn, telling everyone how he had fallen asleep again that day and let the sheep into the meadow and the cow into the corn.

Suddenly a cat walked up on its hind legs, with a little dog. He spoke sharply to Tom.

"Where did you get that fiddle? I believe it's mine."

"No, it's not," said Polly. "And don't talk to Tom like that."

"Ho! So it's Tom the Piper's Son, who learnt to play when he was young, is it?" cried the farmer's wife, who suddenly appeared behind them. "Why, my husband has just gone after him. Didn't he steal a pig of ours and eat it? Yes, he did, the scamp."

"I tell you I'm not Tom the Piper's Son," said Tom.

"Well, there's only one other Tom in Nursery-Rhyme Land, and that's Tommy Tucker," said the farmer's wife. "Sing and show us you are Tommy Tucker."

"I'm not Tommy Tucker, either," said Tom. "And this fiddle doesn't belong to that cat. Tom the Piper's Son gave it to me to hold."

"It is my fiddle!" said the cat. "I used it last night, when the cow jumped over the moon. Then the dish ran away with the spoon, and now there's only me and the little dog left. I put my fiddle under a bush and this morning it was gone. You must have taken it. Shame on you! Who are you, anyway?"

"I'm Tom and she's Polly," said Tom, beginning to be frightened, because by now quite a crowd had collected around them. "We only came here for an adventure. We don't really belong. We'd better go home."

"They don't belong!" cried everyone. "They don't belong. What shall we do with them?"

Up came an old woman wearing a

big bonnet and a shawl. "I'll take them," she said. "I know what to do with naughty children. There's plenty of room in my Shoe!"

Polly gave a squeal.

"I don't want to go with you!" she cried. But the Old Woman had them firmly by the hand. She led them across the market, kicking and struggling. She went down a little street and they came to a field. In the field was the Shoe!

But what an enormous one! It must surely have belonged to a giant, for it was big enough to take at least twenty children! A roof had been built over it, with a chimney. There was a door in one side, and windows too. Many children were playing about in the field outside the Shoe.

"Oh, he's got a fiddle!" cried one little girl. "You must be Tom the Piper's Son? I knew the Old Woman would get you some day. Play to us!"

Crash! One of the windows in the

26

house was suddenly smashed. It made Tom and Polly jump. The Old Woman turned and looked at the suddenly quiet children.

"Who threw that stone?" she said. Nobody answered. The Old Woman was very angry.

"That's the third time this week that window has been broken. Indoors all of you!"

The frightened children ran into the queer shoe house. Tom and Polly went with them. The Old Woman followed, and shut the door with a bang. Polly whispered the rhyme to Tom:

"There was an old woman
who lived in a shoe;
She had so many children
she didn't know what to do;
She gave them some broth
without any bread,
And whipped them all soundly
and put them to bed."

"It isn't fair that we should be kept here," whispered Polly. "I don't want to be whipped and sent to bed. Look – let's run out of the back door."

Tom and Polly dashed out. The Old Woman jumped up and ran after them, but they had a very good start. They ran quickly across the field as fast as their legs would take them. They went through a gate and out into a lane. They saw a stile and climbed over it. Beyond was a cornfield, and Polly saw Little Boy Blue's cow still in the corn.

They took the path and ran across to a little wood. The Old Woman was still after them, and behind her streamed all the children, yelling loudly. Into the wood went Polly and Tom, and soon found a path to follow. After a bit the Old Woman and her children could no longer be heard.

"We're safe," said Polly, "But how are we to get home, Tom? We're quite lost!"

"No, we're not!" said Tom, as he looked around. "Why this is the wood near our house. We shall soon be home!"

"So it is!" cried Polly. "Oh, Tom, whatever will people say when we tell them about our adventure!"

"Nobody will believe us," said Tom. "Nobody! I wonder if it could have been a dream. Do you think it was, Polly?"

"Well, if you still have Tom the Piper's Son's fiddle when we get home, and I have my sixpence, it couldn't be a dream," said Polly.

They were soon home and safe in the kitchen. They looked at one another.

"I've still got the fiddle – and if Tom doesn't come to fetch it, I'm going to learn to play it!" said Tom.

"And I have my sixpence, so it really did happen, Tom. We've been to Nursery-Rhyme Land after all. What an exciting time we've had!"

They had, hadn't they? Look out for the signpost on your walks, if you want to go there, too. But beware of the Old Woman in the Shoe!

• **THE END** •